The Right Touch was inspired by "Jimmy's Bedtime Story," a play that has been performed for thousands of parents and children by the SOAPBox Players of Bellingham, Washington. This volunteer theatre company uses drama to address important issues. A portion of the proceeds from sales of *The Right Touch* will support the work of this organization.

o o O O o o

"I know this sensitive book will help many children."

Barbara Bush
Former First Lady

the right touch

A Read-Aloud Story To Help Prevent
Child Sexual Abuse

Sandy Kleven, LCSW
Illustrations by Jody Bergsma

ILLUMINATION
Arts

PUBLISHING COMPANY, INC.
BELLEVUE, WASHINGTON

To Carmina Marie Kleven,
a new life, a new love
– Sandy Kleven

To innocent children everywhere
– Jody Bergsma

A Note to Parents and Teachers

The Right Touch was developed as a gentle and thoughtful tool for teaching skills to help prevent child sexual abuse. All of us, especially children, need affection and personal contact. However, children should be taught that secret, deceptive, or forced touching is wrong and should be immediately reported to a trusted adult. They should know how to firmly resist when touch becomes inappropriate. Sex offenders admit that compliant children are much more likely to be victimized.

Since approximately eighty percent of those who abuse children are known to the family, it isn't enough to teach "stranger danger." Offenders may be trusted authority figures or even family members. Young victims often feel a sense of complicity and are afraid to tell because they think they will be punished. Offenders use this fear to intimidate children into keeping quiet about abusive incidents.

The Right Touch validates a child's innate warning system. Children generally sense when things aren't "right," so it is important to encourage them to trust their feelings and seek help. Jody Bergsma's *Garden of Children* poster on the back cover can be used to help children visually identify their feelings and emotions.

The illustration on page 23, "Girl's Body, Boy's Body," presents an easy way to teach the names of private body parts. I have omitted labels so parents can choose the words they are most comfortable with.

At what age is it appropriate to teach prevention skills? When a child is able to sit still and pay attention to a story, he or she is old enough for *The Right Touch*. If a child tells you about an abusive situation, I offer the following guidelines:

- Believe the child.
- Assure the child that it was right to tell and that the abuse was not his or her fault.
- Don't confront the accused offender.
- Request assistance from the police, sheriff, or child protection agency.
- Call the Childhelp USA® Hotline at 1-800-4-A-CHILD. Trained counselors are available 24 hours a day for crisis intervention and referrals to counseling agencies and support groups. Literature is available on request. Children and adults may be connected to counselors in 144 languages as needed.
- Use the Internet to find a vast network of resources to help deal with this unfortunate but all-too-common problem. The Childhelp USA® site is a good place to start: *www.childhelpusa.org* or you can e-mail to *help@childhelpusa.org*.

Sandy Kleven, LCSW

When Jimmy's mother tucks him in bed at night, they always talk for awhile. They talk about interesting things, silly things, and serious things. One night she said, "One of my favorite things is tickling your tummy." She tickled him gently, and Jimmy laughed.

"I also like to give you hugs," she said, cuddling him close. "And most of all," she teased, "I like to nibble on your ear." She nuzzled his earlobe and made turkey sounds, "Gibble, gobble, gibble."

Jimmy laughed again. "Stop it, Mom! Stop!"

"Okay," she said. "When you say stop, I always stop, right?"

Jimmy took a deep breath. "I was just kidding! Do it again!"

"Not now," said his mother, "because I want to talk about touching problems."

"What's a touching problem?" he asked.

"If I kept tickling you and tickling you, and I wouldn't stop no matter what you said, that would be a touching problem."

"That would be a mean thing to do," said Jimmy.

She nodded. "There are other kinds of touching problems, too."

"Like when Spot licks me on the face. Yuck!"

"Yes," she said. "Or when a bully gets you down and sits on you and won't let you go."

"That happened to me once," Jimmy agreed.

"It did?" his mom asked. "How did you feel?"

"I was so mad!"

"You sound mad! I'm sure glad you're safe now."

Then Jimmy's mother asked, "Have you ever been tricked?"

"Hmmmm," Jimmy wondered. "Do you mean like when someone says 'Open your mouth and close your eyes, and you will get a big surprise' and the surprise is a worm?"

"Yes," his mom said, "that's what I mean. But there are other tricks, too. Once there was a little girl..."

"Do I know her?" Jimmy asked.

"No, but she is a real person. One day when the little girl was playing outside, a neighbor walked up and said, 'Would you like to come over to my house to see some new baby kittens?'

"Since she knew this person, she went with him. When the girl was inside his house, she looked all around. 'Where are the kittens?' she asked."

The man said, 'If you sit on my lap, I'll show you the kittens.'

"Then the little girl got an uncomfortable feeling. She was about to go home when the man tried to put his hand down her panties."

"He did?" Jimmy asked.

"Yes, he did." Jimmy's mother nodded. "So the little girl ran out of there as fast as she could."

"Did she get away?"

"She ran all the way home and told her mother and father what had happened."

"What did they do to the man?"

"He got into big trouble. What he did is wrong. It's against the law, too. He will have to learn never to try anything like that again."

"Why would somebody want to do that to a little kid, Mom?" asked Jimmy.

"I don't know, honey," his mother answered, shaking her head sadly. "I just know that it does happen sometimes. But if we talk about it, we can help you to be safe."

"Do you remember in the story where the little girl felt uncomfortable?"

Jimmy nodded.

"Lots of kids say they get warning feelings when things are not safe. Some children say it's a nervous feeling. Others say that their tummies feel upset. So be sure to pay attention when warning feelings tell you to watch out."

"Does it feel like when you're gonna throw up?" asked Jimmy.

"It might." Jimmy's mother smiled at him. "Or you could feel tickly and prickly like a nervous cat. Warning feelings are like a safety whistle."

Jimmy's mother looked at him and smiled. "Your whole body, from head to toe, is private and belongs to you. Some parts of your body are extra personal and private. We wear bathing suits when we go swimming so we can cover up our private places. Private places are off limits for touching unless there's a good reason."

"What if I have a sore on my bottom?" Jimmy asked.

"What do you think?"

"I'd want you to fix it."

"In a case like that, it would be okay for Dad or me to take care of things. It's also okay for a doctor or nurse to check you all over and give you a shot in your bottom if you need one. It's okay to change a baby's diaper. And, of course, babies and small children need help with washing and drying."

"Now let's say someone was trying to touch you under your clothes. What would you do?"

"I'd want them to stop."

"The first thing you do is *tell* that person to stop. This might be hard to say to someone who is bigger and older than you, so I think we should practice. Can you say 'Stop it. I don't like that'?"

Jimmy repeated in a loud voice, "Stop it. I don't *like* that!!"

"Good job," said his mother. "You sounded like you really meant it. I want you to remember that no one has the right to touch private parts of your body without a good reason, not even Dad or me."

"If there isn't a good reason, say no, just like we practiced. I know that could be hard, because kids think they should do whatever they are told. But some people are pretty mixed up. Sometimes grown-ups, babysitters, and bigger kids try to trick children into secret touching games that might seem like fun at first. If something like this happens to you, don't be afraid to tell me, even if it is supposed to be a secret. And remember, touching problems are never a child's fault."

"I would always tell," Jimmy yawned. "But you know what?"

"What, honey?" his mom asked.

"Can I please have a drink of water?"

Jimmy's mother smiled. "I'll get you a drink of water," she said, "but you will remember what we talked about won't you?"

"Yeah, Mom, I'll remember. Say no. Get away. No matter what happens, tell someone. And it's not the kid's fault."

o o O o o

"Kisses and cuddles I like a lot,
but when I say no, please touch me not."

Sandy Kleven, LCSW

A licensed clinical social worker, Sandy Kleven has worked assisting families for more than twenty years. As a grief counselor, she often traveled by snowmobile to the remote villages of Alaska. Sandy's activities in sexual abuse prevention include developing and testing prevention curriculums; presenting workshops for parents, teachers, and children; and creating an Emmy Award-winning docudrama, *The Touching Problem*. For five years she served as director of the SOAPBox Players, an acclaimed prevention theatre group in Bellingham, Washington.

Sandy's dramatic monologue *Holy Land* was published in *Alaska Quarterly Review*, Spring 2005. She also writes a regular parenting column in the *Delta Discovery*. For media interviews, speaking engagements and workshops, contact skleven@ak.net.

o · O · Ö · O · o

Jody Bergsma

An internationally renowned artist, Jody Bergsma has been a professional illustrator since her mid-teens. Between frequent national tours, she lives near Bellingham, Washington, where she was named the city's outstanding businessperson in 1995.

Each of Jody's books has won at least one national award. *The Right Touch* received the 1999 Benjamin Franklin Award in the parenting category. *Dreambirds* was selected Best Children's Book of 1998 by the Coalition of Visionary Retailers. *Sky Castle* received a 1999 Children's Choice Award from the Children's Book Council. *Dragon* and *The Little Wizard* were named Best Children's Book of 2000 and 2001 respectively by the Coalition of Visionary Retailers. Her latest book, *Faerie* was named Children's Book of the Year by *ForeWord Magazine* in 2003.

Jody's limited edition prints and other gift items are sold in gift stores nationwide. For more information call 1-800-BERGSMA or visit www.bergsma.com.

ILLUMINATION

Arts

PUBLISHING COMPANY, INC.

P.O. Box 1865, Bellevue, Washington 98009
Tel: 425-644-7185 ❖ 888-210-8216 (orders only) ❖ Fax: 425-644-9274
E-mail: liteinfo@illumin.com   www.illumin.com

Library of Congress Cataloging-in-Publication Data

Kleven, Sandy.
    The right touch : a read aloud story to help prevent child sexual abuse / Sandy
Kleven ; illustrations by Jody Bergsma.
       p. cm.
    Summary: As a way of teaching her little boy about sexual abuse, a mother
tells him the story of a child who was lured into the neighbor's house to see some
non-existent kittens.
    ISBN 0-935699-10-4 (hardcover)
    [1. Child sexual abuse--Fiction.] I. Bergsma, Jody, ill.
II. Title.
PZ7.K678388Ri   1998
[E]--dc21   98-11556
                                                CIP
                                                AC

Fifth Printing

Published in the United States of America
Printed in Singapore by Tien Wah Press

Book Designer:
Molly Murrah, Murrah & Company, Kirkland, WA

Cover Designer:
Peri Poloni, Knockout Design, Placerville, CA

Illumination Arts is a member of Publishers in Partnership –
replanting our nation's forests.